# FEATHERLIGHT

## ALSO BY MONALISA FOSTER

Stand-alone works in the **Ravages of Honor** universe:

*Novels*

Ravages of Honor

*Novellas*

Enemy Beloved

Featherlight

Dominion (upcoming)

*Short Story*

Bonds of Duty and Love (available April 7, 2020)

—Short Fiction—

The Greatest Crime (upcoming)

The Heretic

Catching the Dark

Bellona's Gift

Promethea Invicta: A Novella

Cooper

Equality

Dolus Magnus: The Great Hoax

Collective Responsibility

—Non-fiction—

Rejection 101: A Writer's Guide

# FEATHERLIGHT

## A RAVAGES OF HONOR NOVELLA

## MONALISA FOSTER

*For all who serve.*

# INTRODUCTION

One of the most common questions I've gotten from those who read **Ravages of Honor** is, "What are the *donai* women like?"

Like so much about the *donai's* world, the scope of **Ravages** didn't really let me address that question. The **Ravages** universe and its inhabitants are too big, too detailed, too deep to be fully developed in one novel, even a 150,000-word one.

But the story of Lady Yedon did give me the perfect opportunity to answer this question, at least for one *donai*. Lady Yedon was introduced in **Ravages** during Galen's flashback to the first time he met Emperor Thán Kabrin.

If you've read **Ravages**, some of the world-building details are repeated here (for those that have not). If you have not read **Ravages**, it's my sincerest hope that you will.

Either way, know that this novella stands alone as its own story. And that, unlike **Ravages**, it is a dark one.

# CHAPTER ONE

*V*aleria stormed through the arched hallways leading from the swordhall to the Sovereign's Suite as though she were some elemental force of nature. Her blonde hair was darkened by sweat. She swept it out of her eyes and tucked it behind her ear.

Barefoot, she strode across intricate mosaics, cutting through shadows cast by carved, stone titans. Lightning split the sky, hurling blinding flashes of light at a universe gone wrong. The storm brewing outside was nothing compared to the tides of emotions she was caught in. They sent her crashing against unyielding cliffs and then sucked her back only to smash her anew.

Valeria was losing her strength and agility—an unbearable travesty. She'd not only lost the sparring session with her men, but she'd emerged bruised and battered. Healing was taking longer than it should have. Had it been a real fight, her enemies could've finished her off despite the nanites that gave her kind—the *donai*—their incredible healing ability.

The doors slid aside and she entered the ante-chamber. Lanterns floated down from the ceiling, casting a soft glow in the spartan chamber. Intricately carved panels covered the walls, deceptively hiding the ante-chamber's main function: a kill-box. No enemy could pass through this chamber into the ones beyond where they might catch her unaware. Everything in the room, from the lanterns, to the tiles, to the panels was made of utility fog. Nanites stood ready to change form as needed, depending on the threat level.

A sword rack protruded from the column just inside the main chamber. She shed the killing sword and placed it on the rack, but the short sword remained within reach even as she stepped out of the *hakama* and shrugged out of the wide-sleeved jacket. They landed on the tiles as she made her way past over-stuffed couches and low tables. She had no attendants—not today, not tomorrow, not as long as she was like this. The fewer people who knew of her growing weakness, the better.

The chamber presence had dulled the mirrored walls. It knew that she could no longer bear the sight of her body. The *donai* may have started out human, still conforming in general appearance, but she could not look at the changes she'd undergone. Her softness disgusted her. Even the swell of her belly was false, mocking.

It was different for the men. Larger, taller, the *donai* men merely looked like enhanced versions of their progenitors. Only the layered amber irises of augmented eyes and the points of their ears gave them away. But the differences between humans and *donai* were truly pronounced in the women of her sub-species.

It was those differences that had been offending her for some time. Her musculature had become less defined, weak and prone to damage. There were times when the new weakness of her muscle fibers turned her stomach. Even the density of her bones had changed. She was no longer able to tolerate impacts without risking fracture and breakage: slow-to-heal fracture and breakage.

She entered the dimly lit bathing chamber with its simulated stone walls, its simulated sky, its simulated peace.

Caretaker nanites had turned the bath water opaque with their shimmer. They glittered and swirled in her wake as she lowered herself into the steam so the extra dose of nanotech could accelerate her healing. Maybe they'd even wash off the stench of failure. Unbearable

2

weakness resonated deep within her heart, increasing the pressure in her tear ducts.

All normal, she'd been told.

All part of the change.

She breathed through the sudden frailty and eased into the giant tub. Warmth seeped into aching muscles, a lingering caress that made her crave touch—real touch—in a way she never had before.

Despite her young, talented physician's warnings, his agonizingly detailed explanations, she'd never imagined the true extent of the consequences she'd agreed to bear. Ever since she'd acquired him, her pursuit of an heir had been single-minded, but in moments like this, she questioned her resolve. And his loyalty.

*When there is no penalty for failure, failure proliferates.*

It was so very tempting to assign failure to him and his methods. But she hadn't become the sovereign of her House by ignoring facts. It was a fact that *donai* women had been engineered *for* infertility. She'd been fortunate to find someone willing to even attempt altering that engineering.

"Galen Karamat requesting entry," the chamber presence announced in a soothing, male tone. It had been designed to mimic the best-trained majordomos in every way, from syntax to the way it antic- ipated her needs. And unlike a human majordomo, it was utterly loyal, incapable of gossip or spying, all things which had become an increasing matter of concern over the last few months.

"Is he alone?" she asked, scrubbing at the aching bruise blooming on her forearm.

"Yes, Lady Yedon."

"Let him in."

Unhurried footsteps approached. Her pet physician was tall for a human. When they stood face to face, she could look him straight in the eyes, which was in itself an interesting experience. Not many humans dared. Not after the *donai* had revolted, turned on their human creators and built an Imperium where all humans were chattel.

Strange gray eyes on Galen. Dark hair and strong masculine features despite being clean shaven—and human. He wore a gray tunic with a high collar and darker gray trousers and boots. His collar bore insignia identifying him as a physician of the Court, and as her property. His thin frame gave him a frail appearance, a deceptive one. What he lacked in strength and size he made up for with intelligence and persistence. She needed to remember that.

"My lady," he said, his voice even. Too even.

For weeks, her *donai* senses had been deteriorating. She could no longer see the heat gradients on his skin, hear the betraying cadence of his heartbeat, or smell the hormones seeping through his pores. She could call in one of her *donai* armsmen and have him read Galen for her, but that would expose her shortcoming and call her abilities into question. Eventually her men would lose faith in her and she could no longer lead them.

She waited.

No bow.

He didn't like bending his spine, this human, and whenever they were alone, he did not. He knew she'd tolerate his defiance in private and never made the mistake of not giving her the proper obeisance in public where she would be forced to act. She had no doubt that it was going to cost him someday. He'd fail to properly kowtow to some *donai* lord who wouldn't tolerate the transgression.

The Imperium had only spared the most docile, passive humans, and still took great pleasure in eliminating all who showed any tendency to become the dominant species once again. Perhaps a lesson imparted at her hand would be a mercy, for she would merely punish, not kill, but she could not bring herself to teach it. It was a dangerous sentiment, one she should not indulge in, but did, yet again. He was too valuable and she trusted him. Not since she'd reached adulthood had she looked at a human with anything one might call regard.

Galen reached into the pocket of his uniform and withdrew a medical rover. The palm-sized disk lit up, swelled into a sphere and floated towards her. He launched two others and sent them her way.

Diagnostic beams sliced the air with a pale blue shimmer, casting lines across her body. A rover submerged, swirling around her, as a holographic projection detailing all the damage she'd taken, coalesced in front of him.

He raised a brow, casting a judging gaze her way. "Have you changed your mind?"

So smug, so arrogant, as if he was begging for that lesson.

Her short sword was within reach. Even in her weakened state, she could still move much faster than he could react.

All it would take was a few cuts—nothing fatal, even for a human. The rovers and nanites would heal him readily enough. Unlike the *donai*, whose obedience to anyone they recognized as a leader was ingrained and instinctual, certain humans seemed to need gentle reminders.

"No," she said. "I haven't changed my mind."

Shrinking rovers returned to Galen's hand. He pocketed them as he held her gaze. "Your behavior suggests otherwise."

"I stopped before they pushed me too far. The lingering bruises, the aches, are proof of that."

*Aren't they?*

This was the other side of the unfair coin her kind had been dealt by these same humans. If she took too much damage, her nanites would compensate and undo all the things Galen had done to make her fertile. Battle-driven hormones would return her muscles and bones to their former strength. The nanites would burn the fat she'd managed to accumulate and she would never ovulate. The handful of eggs she *might* have would never be fertilized. And then all of these months of vulnerability she'd had to suffer would be for nothing.

Without a proper *donai* heir, it was only a matter of time before the emperor took her House away from her.

A pained look flashed across Galen's face as he swept the hologram away.

"You were lucky this time," he said dryly.

She sighed and let her head fall back. Tremors propagated an unexpected release in tension. It had been so difficult to hold back, to let her armsmen win, to walk that fine line that might lead them to question her fitness or her ability to lead them.

"Your *donai* are bound to notice the changes," Galen continued. "Why not just tell them what you are doing?"

"As soon as they see me as a potential sexual partner, they'll compete for that 'honor' and tear my dominion apart."

"You do realize you will need them to—"

"*Them?* Do you see me as human already?"

She must've let more anger than she'd intended color her voice. There was a flare of emotion from Galen. Fear maybe. Or anger. She couldn't be sure. Humans learned to hide the reactions they could control. The scent clue was gone almost as quickly as it had appeared.

"No, my lady," he said, lifting his chin, making no attempt to hide his pride. "You told me you were willing to do anything and multiple partners would increase your chances of conceiving."

"No," she said, rising, and strode out of the water, stopping only to pick up the short sword. She passed through the drying field and walked straight on to her bedchamber.

"How can you still not understand us?" she asked. "You who know so much about us."

"I understand, my lady," he said, following, maintaining a respectful—for him—distance.

She slipped into the dark blues of the ship-fatigues she'd set out prior to the sparring session. They were too form-fitting, betraying her softening physique. Robes would've been better. Maybe she could become one of those *donai* sovereigns whose affectations tended towards the anachronistic. Why not? A return to tradition. The emperor would love that.

Galen cleared his throat. "Have you selected the father?"

"Someone outside of my House." This was essential. It would prevent infighting and she could remain unattainable to all those whose fealty she commanded.

"Someone not of the peerage," she added. Another necessity—a costly one. Someone who would not challenge her was necessarily someone who also brought her no assets, no allies.

"Someone fertile," he said as a smile lifted the corners of his mouth.

6

She froze in the middle of sealing her tunic.

It was humans, humans like him, who'd created the *donai* to fight their wars and deliberately made them infertile so they'd have no competing loyalties.

It was humans like him who'd not been content with merely making the *donai* stronger and faster and smarter. In order to alter their behaviors, they'd had to meddle with their genetics as well, and what better model than a wolf-pack to ensure the loyalty of one's soldiers *and* limit their numbers.

"Do I amuse you?" she asked.

His face reddened and he was silent for a moment as though considering his words.

"I did warn you," he said softly. "Once you conceive, the—"

"Yes, yes—I will be vulnerable." She waved his concern away as she finished dressing. "Once I am pregnant, my *donai* will be all the protection I need."

There was pity in his eyes.

"Galen, don't ever look at me like that again."

He lowered his gaze. "Yes, my lady."

There was contrition in his voice. Barely. She doubted she'd see it in his eyes, but she didn't look, allowing him his petty defiances.

She needed no human's pity.

His knowledge, yes. That was essential. She'd prefer having his loyalty as well, because she looked upon him as part of her pack—a fatal flaw. The Imperium took a dim view of such proclivities, considered them a fault, a remnant of the human evils that had turned the *donai* into disposable tools of war, ready and willing to sacrifice themselves to protect the very humans that enslaved them.

Galen was still before her, head slightly bent, gaze downcast, his deference an ill-fitting garment. As a sovereign, as *donai*, that deference should've pleased her. Instead, it only reminded her how much she needed him.

*We're inexorably bound, humans and* donai. *No wonder the emperor hates humans so.*

7

# CHAPTER TWO

*L*ong silken sleeves hid Valeria's hands as her fingertips dug into her throne's armrests. In the last two months, she'd bowed to necessity, donning formal robes to hide her body's softening and taking increasingly aggressive measures to mask her scent.

Behind her, Galen stood in the shadows, an I-told-you-so look lingering on his face.

Beside her, her armsmen bristled, unmoving, obedient to her order that they not interfere. They obeyed, holding still with great effort as one of their own took a well-deserved beating and someone with no fealty to her House yielded a weapon in her presence.

Blood dripped off her guest's sword as his opponent—one of her own *donai*—retreated, stumbling and scrabbling after the sword he'd dropped. Maho—younger and faster than her master-swordsman guest —was losing not only to experience, but his own panic. It flowed off him in waves, permeating the air with a stench that assaulted even her dulled senses.

Maho's right arm was a mangled mess. It dangled uselessly at his side as he recovered his sword, barely managing a left-handed block. Sparks flew and the clash of metal echoed. They spun, engaging at speeds that would've been a blur to the human eye, slowing only for intermittent seconds.

A *donai* called Palleton, House Dobromil's master-swordsman, moved with unbelievable speed given his huge size and advanced age. His skin was dark like mahogany and his gold irises were fully dilated. Short gray hair was clipped close to his scalp. It framed prominent ear-points and the weathered features of a battle-hardened veteran. Wrapped in the formal robes of his House, Palleton was a blur of black and red as he wielded his sword.

No matter what Maho did, Palleton's blade pierced his defenses, sweeping out arc after arc, carving the symbol for "fool" into the young *donai's* chest with each deliberate stroke.

"Stop!"

She winced. Her contralto voice was gone, replaced by something with a higher pitch.

Palleton froze, sword raised with both hands beside his right ear, in a setup for the killing blow.

Instead of obeying, Maho used the pause to sweep a cut across Palleton's abdomen, slicing through his robes and the top layer of skin beneath them.

She held her breath as Palleton leapt over Maho and slashed through the back of his opponent's calves. Maho dropped to his knees, but scored another shallow cut—a lucky but clumsy move—as he rolled and went down. Maho held Palleton's gaze, raising his chin defiantly, daring the elder *donai* to finish him.

Valeria stood. "I gave the order to stop."

That Palleton was holding back instead of separating Maho's head from his body was a testament to his control. She wished he would just do it and spare her the need to punish Maho's foolishness.

The sword descended, stopping at Maho's neck. The young fool still would not drop his gaze. Such utter folly. What had gotten into him? In all of her armsmen? They'd been slowly losing their discipline.

House Dobromil and House Yedon may not have been the closest allies, but Palleton was here by invitation. One's armsmen weren't supposed to challenge an honored guest, at least not without good reason.

Her heels clicked down the steps as she approached the pair, stopping just short of the main floor with its blood-streaked tiles.

"Eyes down," she ordered.

Maho's gaze darted to hers and still he waited for three heartbeats before he lowered his gaze, and then finally, his chin.

"There you go, Swordmaster," she said, using her most soothing tone. "He surrenders."

With a snarl, Palleton stepped back and cleared the blood groove. He never took his gaze off his defeated opponent.

Still on his knees, breathing raggedly, Maho cradled his useless arm to his chest, trying to hide the already healing symbol. Valeria knew that it would never fade from his memory. Young men gave such things too much power. There was no way for him to emerge from this with his honor intact.

Still, she could not give the order to end his life.

*Sentiment. Weak, foolish, sentiment.* It was going to be the end of her.

"As you say, my lady," Palleton said, sheathing his sword. His tone said that he too had expected her to let him end Maho's life.

Unlike Maho, Palleton had shown good discipline, leaving the decision to her, even when he had every right to take the young *donai's* life.

Her armsmen rushed forward to help Maho stand. Galen trailed behind them. When Galen reached down to help, Maho shook him off, insisting he could stand on his own. He collapsed as the muscles of his damaged calves pushed through skin that hadn't had enough time to heal.

A fresh torrent of blood gushed onto the tile.

With a flick of the wrist, she signaled her armsmen into action. They bracketed Maho and dragged him off.

Galen's gray-eyed gaze met Palleton's for an instant before he hurried after her *donai*. With one last questioning look, Galen pulled the doors closed behind him.

11

She was alone with this armed, towering stranger, in a room permeated with blood and testosterone.

Palleton's silent gaze was very intense, resting on her hair. She no longer gathered it in a peer's queue behind her neck, but had left it loose to form a soft golden halo around her face and cascade to her shoulders. A change in hairstyle made it easier to attribute the changes to her face.

Palleton's gaze skated down to her breasts, her waist. The pale rose color she'd chosen for her robes masked the feminine curves. Enough layers, textures, and patterns and she could camouflage the changes that, with each passing week, made her look less and less a warrior.

"I didn't realize House Yedon's relations with House Dobromil were good enough for us to be alone," Palleton said, his voice a soft, caressing rumble.

She resisted the urge to inhale his scent, that deep, dark, earthy musk that hung around him like a cloud.

"You have a message for me, do you not, Swordmaster?"

She smiled, inching closer, basking in that cloud, very much aware of the way it tugged at her and pulled her in.

"I thought it best I hear it without the benefit of an audience," she added.

The pulse at his neck had slowed from frenzied pounding to steady rhythm. Sweat trickled down his cheek, a tiny rivulet of salt and dizzying pheromones.

He grunted, a small sound laced with amusement. "Without having to worry about any more of your men challenging me, you mean."

Her smile faded. She met his gaze.

"The passions of young men," she said. "I shall see to it that he makes a proper apology."

"And will you also tell him what's driving his passions?"

The words plucked her from the miasma of pheromones and plunged her into cold, bitter reality.

*He knew.*

Of course he knew. Lord Dobromil would have, no doubt, told him. He'd not have sent his swordmaster as a mere errand boy.

"What is Dobromil's answer?" she asked.

"*I* am Lord Dobromil's answer," Palleton said, as he crossed his arms and met her gaze, measure for measure.

Humiliation burned its way up her neck, across her face, right into the tips of her ears, a throbbing, pulsing ache with a life of its own. How dare he, another lord's vassal, stand before her—the sovereign of her own House—as an equal?

"You?" she demanded, closing in.

She stopped just short of the bloodied tiles. The crimson liquid was thick and rich with iron and the tang of copper. Pheromones rose from it. To this her senses had not dulled. Would not dull. She held her breath, forced into silence by its lack, until she could bear it no more and stepped around the puddle.

"Everyone knows you've been here," she said. "It wouldn't take much to figure out who fathered my heir."

"It will be even more apparent when I take my place as your consort," he said calmly, continuing to scrutinize her, his layered irises contracting and dilating.

Such audacity, to use his augmented vision to peer into her body as if she were human. It wasn't just a breach of protocol, it was insulting. It made her feel like prey. This close, she couldn't hide anything from him, no matter how many layers of fabric she wore.

"Consort?" she asked, moving in close enough to touch him.

She couldn't help herself. She should have been fleeing the room, getting as far away from him as she could.

"I did not ask Dobromil for a consort."

"Then you should consider taking a human lover."

He caught her hand an instant before it could strike his cheek. Oversized and rough, it remained wrapped around her wrist, a dark shadow over her pale skin. She was shaking. With rage. With shame. With desire.

A human? A human lover was useless to her. Some *donai* could father children on human women, but no female *donai* had ever conceived with a human.

She struggled to free her wrist, but he wouldn't allow it. He forced her palm open and swept his nose over the inside of her hand, inhaling deeply.

"You ask for my lord's help and then strike at me, first through that young fool competing for your favor, and now like this?"

"I did no such thing. Let. Me. Go."

The grin on his mahogany face was cold, the amber eyes glowing like embers. "Make me."

He knew she couldn't, not the way she was now. Fertility had its price. Galen had warned her, again and again, and she'd been certain she was ready for the cost. Anything was worth an heir, she'd told him. Even her pride, she'd insisted. And now the bill was due and she was unwilling to pay it.

"You'll never make it back alive," she said, drawing a blade from her robes, placing its tip at his midriff where Maho had sliced through the layered black and red of Dobromil's colors.

As he looked down his smile became cold and hard.

His gaze rose slowly as he drew her closer and grabbed her chin, ignoring the blade. She tried to jerk away, but his grip was firm, forcing her to meet his gaze. He grunted in amusement as blood trickled over the blade in her trembling hand.

He leaned in, his scent suffocating, drowning, clawing at her and her will. Weak-kneed, she dared not move, nor breathe, nor blink.

"I will not give you what you seek," he whispered and let her go.

Unbalanced, she stumbled backwards, blade shaking so hard she feared dropping it.

He swept out a bow worthy of the Imperial Court. The shallow cut to his abdomen was already healed, the potent scent of his blood fading quickly.

Her vision misted. "I have not dismissed you, Swordmaster."

"No, my lady, you have not."

VALERIA TUCKED the blade back into the fold of her robe, lest she drop it.

Palleton's footsteps receded, rhyming against those of someone coming towards the throne room. She recognized the approaching pattern and braced herself with a cleansing breath. She was going to have words with the person responsible for allowing Owyn Tolek, the emperor's own spy-master, to come anywhere near Dobromil's lackey, much less allow them to pass each other in the same hallway.

Valeria whirled, heading for the comfort of her throne, stepping around the spilled blood. She cleared her head with a shake and blinked her eyes dry.

Tolek didn't wait to be announced, invading her domain with all the arrogance of one who had the emperor's favor. His vestments shouted his allegiance to the emperor's House.

Short for a *donai* male, and he nevertheless had the signature amber irises. Unlike other *donai*, his layered pupils boasted both silver and gold. That anomaly and the pearl-white hair made him stand out. His leaner, sinewy physique, without the typical *donai* bulk was by design. There was no advantage to a spy-master who stood out the way he did, except for one thing—he could pass for human, and often did.

The long fingers of his hand were wrapped loosely around a baton-like cylinder.

"Reduced to courier today, are you?" Valeria asked.

He gave her a blood-curdling smile. His eyes changed color, both of his layered pupils swirling to black as his hair flushed through a palette of color and settled on a dull brown.

"Don't worry," he said. "It'll take him a while to realize why the 'human' courier didn't smell quite right. *If* he realizes it at all. All that blood. He seemed quite ... agitated."

"One of my *donai* challenged him."

"And lost."

Tolek's eyes flashed back to amber-shrouded metals as color leached out of his hair.

Valeria knew that there was a price for his modifications—his senses weren't quite up to *donai* standards—but she still needed to keep him at a distance.

It would not do to have the emperor know what she had done. He might well intervene, sending her someone of his own choosing, someone loyal to him.

The thought of a pair-bond with Dobromil's lackey was abhorrent enough. A pair-bond with the emperor's would be worse.

She rested her elbow on the armrest, propping her chin so she could rub it against her hand. Palleton's scent lingered on her skin. She needed a bath. A long one.

And the chamber needed to be scrubbed as well. All the blood and testosterone were driving her to distraction, already making her reconsider Dobromil's offer.

"We've taken House Hevonen down," Tolek said, watching her through narrowed eyes.

She used a shrug to hide a deep draw of Palleton's scent from her wrist, before answering with, "Months ago, according to reports. Is that what you've come to tell me?"

He tossed the cylinder between them. It hovered above the pooled blood as a hologram fountained above.

A lone gas giant circled its distant sun. Dozens of satellites circled the giant sphere of gas with its hundred or so bands of swirling color. Navigation lines appeared to trace satellite orbits, and with them, telemetry. Blooms of data popped up alongside every piece of rock.

"Do you recognize it?" Tolek asked.

"Should I?"

"Then how about this?"

He manipulated the hologram, zeroing in on a moon with an atmosphere. Above it, a ship orbited, one with House Hevonen's sigil —a screeching raptor—still visible despite the blast marks etching its unhealed hull.

She shifted in her seat, leaning towards the projection, mouth suddenly dry. "I know nothing of this."

That blood-curdling smile returned. "So it's incompetence that allowed a known fugitive to raid in your territory, rather than collusion with a fallen House. The emperor will be so pleased."

Tolek's words were a reminder, that for the emperor, excuses did not matter. She should have chosen her words more carefully. The damned blood. The pheromones. They were interfering with her ability to think. She needed to put Tolek back in his place.

Valeria bolted upright. "Watch your tongue. It may grow back by the time you return to imperial space, but I will still enjoy cutting it out."

"Ah," he said, "there's the Lady Yedon I know. For a moment you had me worried. Cavorting with House Dobromil can have such lingering effects—none of them to the emperor's taste."

"I'll have this Hevonen renegade taken care of," she assured him.

The detailed reports of House Hevonen's downfall had made their way into her hands. If chasing down some Hevonen retainers pleased the emperor, then so be it.

Tolek's eyebrow rose as he made a slicing motion that collapsed the floating images. As the cylinder dropped to the floor, he tilted his head slightly, nostrils flaring.

The blood on the floor was like a crumbling wall between them, one she must not allow him to breach.

"The emperor would prefer to make an example of this pirate," Tolek said. "He would prefer your 'delicate' touch. Otherwise we'd have taken our own ships and obliterated the entire planetary system ourselves."

From the way he watched her, she could tell he was probing for weakness, seeking an outburst. He too suspected, baiting her with his choice of words. She looked down at him—on him—from *her* throne.

"After notifying you of our intent, of course," he added. "We would never dream of crossing House Yedon's territory without proper notice."

"Oh yes, I'm certain these images," she gestured to the cylinder, casting his attention back to it and the pool of blood, "were captured from outside our sovereign space."

"We had to be sure," Tolek said.

She took a deep breath. He didn't give off any of the dizzying pheromones that affected her so these days. It made it easy to present him with a congenial smile.

"Tell the emperor that I will give it my personal attention."

"He will be so pleased." His bow was clipped and not as deep as protocol demanded.

"And Tolek," she said as he turned to leave.

"Yes, Lady Yedon."

There were words she didn't want to speak. Another sign of weakness and sentiment she could not afford.

"Dobromil's lackey," she said. "I would take no offense at his demise."

Tolek's lips stretched into a genuine smile as he transitioned to a human façade.

# CHAPTER THREE

*V*aleria gathered the length of her hair tight, containing it behind her neck, in a folded imitation of a peer's proper queue. Tolek's visit had provided her with an excuse for the changes in her appearance: a secret mission for the emperor.

Her senior armsman had been skeptical, but accepted the explanation. He too suspected. That was clear when he quietly reassigned only pair-bonded *donai* to her personal detail. They would show no interest in her, no matter how many pheromones her body pumped out. She'd accepted the changes without comment, secretly grateful for the gesture.

Valeria finished dressing and donned her sword and sidearm just as Galen entered.

"My lady, I have the test results you requested."

His tone, and the stiffness of his posture were a warning. She adjusted the seams of her robe without cringing, without betraying any sense of expectation.

"How many more do I have left?" she asked, a slight tremor creeping in, betraying her fears.

"It's hard to sa—"

"How many, Galen?"

"Two. Maybe three," he said. "Maybe ... one."

*One egg.*

Her heart clenched painfully in her chest.

Galen was honest. She'd give him that. Painfully honest. Another human might have lied, given her false hope out of the desire to appease, to remain in her favor.

"My lady, I still think one of your *donai* is the most logical solution."

"I know you do, Galen."

She picked up a flat sheet of crystal that came to life at her touch. It revealed the mission ship's manifest. She scrolled through it and signed off on the log by pressing her thumb to a shimmering spot in the center of the sheet.

"Will you reconsider?" he asked.

"When I'm done with my mission for the emperor, yes."

The idea of a consort wasn't as abhorrent to her as it had been when she'd turned down Dobromil's lackey. One of her own *donai*, one already sworn to her, would at least owe allegiance to no one else. It would wreak havoc on her chain of command, throw everything into chaos, but with a little bit of luck, she'd have an heir.

"You shouldn't be doing this," Galen whispered, studying his boots. "This mission is a waste of time you don't have."

She made a rude noise and in a mocking tone, said, "I'm so sorry Sire, but I cannot obey you because I'm too busy seducing my men and forging unsanctioned alliances."

Galen cleared his throat. "Then I should attend you."

Over all these months, through all the painful changes, the surges of emotions she couldn't control, Galen had become her accomplice, her confidant. She'd developed a certain affection for him, one that would no doubt fade once this was all over and she returned to normal. She'd have to send him away then. He'd be a constant reminder of failure, of a promise unfulfilled.

"No," she said without a trace of doubt.

Some of the *donai* were already suspicious that she'd taken Galen as a lover. Taking him as her sole companion on this mission would only confirm their fears. It would not end well for him.

He accepted her answer with a sigh and made to leave, only to change his mind.

"You can no longer engage another *donai* in personal combat," he said. "You do understand that, don't you?"

"I understand it very well. That's why I stopped training with my *donai*, why even now they suspect my condition. But, I can take the pirate's head without engaging him directly. The emperor won't care that I incapacitated him before taking his head instead of taking him in honorable combat."

What little she could read of Galen now said that he did not approve. Had he forgotten who she was? Had he really thought she would change so much just because of the physical transformation? She was still, and would always be, *donai*, even if she had traded her combat readiness for a time.

"Galen, do you know how many heads I've brought the emperor?"

He pressed his lips into a tight line. "No, Lady Yedon."

"I stopped counting at one hundred and fifty," she said matter-of-factly.

With a flash of anger, his gaze rose to meet hers.

"Did they deserve it?" he demanded.

She turned to face him. "What?"

"Did they deserve a death sentence?"

"You forget yourself, Galen," she said, as she crossed the distance between them.

He held his ground.

She placed her hand gently on his cheek. It was smooth and slightly colder than she'd expected.

His gray gaze searched hers.

*Galen, those eyes will be the death of you*, she wanted to say. Instead, she said, "You truly have no concept of what it means to be *donai*, do you? Of what our oaths mean?"

"Oaths of blind obedience. Truly, my lady, would *you* obey an order to kill your own child?"

The question made her blink. She stood there, jaw agape at the absurdity of the thought, her hand leaving his cheek to stray to her abdomen.

"Of course not," she said, backing away.

"That is why your emperor took down House Hevonen," he reminded her.

She gave him her back and took a calming breath. "The order was for House Hevonen's human concubines and *their* children."

"*And* the *donai* that they made them with," Galen added.

THE EMPEROR WANTS the renegade's head, Valeria reminded herself, not another pile of rocks orbiting a star not worth naming.

The system already had an impressive number of asteroid belts and comets. Something ancient had pummeled the inner terrestrial planets to rubble. All that debris started giving the ship's navigation system fits as soon as her well-armed interceptor punched through the system's transit point.

For a pirate, the choice of system was a good one.

Far from the bulk of House Yedon's holdings, it was, at best, a backwater. The system had four known phase-shift transit-points. It was an ideal choice, giving him escape routes and the means to double back. It was far enough into her territory that other Houses would think twice about pursuing him here as long as he kept to pettier targets—which he had.

Tinia—someone *had* bothered to name the gas giant—had an impressive collection of satellites, ranging from captured asteroids to a large moon with a spectacular ocean, hundreds of islands, and a solitary continent. There was even a ruin, a remnant of an abandoned colony.

An out-dated, vague, imperial report had concluded that there was enough fauna and flora to support a small settlement indefinitely.

Had that been the pirate's original intent? To go to ground and disappear?

Why risk calling attention to himself with petty raids? Why not run for the Outer Regions? Or take refuge with a House strong enough to remain in open rebellion?

Hevonen's ship wasn't in the system and there no sign of activity on the ground. According to her sensors, her approached remained undetected.

She brought the ship down some distance from the ruin and tucked the interceptor into the shelter of a grotto, then made her way on foot.

With her chameleon-suit covering her from head to toe, she could blend into the night. The surrounding air was even warm enough that as long as she didn't overexert herself, her heat-signature would remain close to ambient.

She'd left her swords behind.

As she'd promised Galen, she had no intention of physically engaging any *donai*. She had been trained to infiltrate and assassinate, a skill not solely dependent on strength or speed.

Above, the herd of moons orbiting Tinia reflected not only the system's distant star but light from the gas giant itself, casting split shadows that slipped and shifted at the edges of her vision, giving them an illusion of motion.

She moved forward, ignoring the distracting plays of light and dark.

Once she was at the perimeter of the ruin she launched a handful of insect-like drones. They spread out, tight-beaming their data to the chameleon-suit's form-fitting hood. A small portion of the ruin had been repaired and a shielded generator thrummed softly into the whisper-quiet night.

The drones flew to the structure, slipped through cracks in the ancient stone, and flitted from room to room. With eye motions, she flipped through their transmission, but they revealed no signs of people and no additional energy signatures. Smart of the pirate, resorting to such primitivism. If only he'd have forgone that generator...

She continued through the arch of a dilapidated side-gate. Its hinges remained, but whatever had served as a door had rotted away long ago.

An empty, crumbling fountain had been overtaken by bioluminescent moss and night-blooming flowers. A cloud of floating light hovered over the blooms, coaxing their pollen pods to open with trailing strands of silk.

Moon-split shadows slid over the courtyard, weaving across weeds and cobblestones.

Valeria ghosted along the dressed stone wall. She kept to shadows as she made her way along the perimeter of the courtyard towards a pair of adjoining rooms that might have been tasked as quarters.

Her heel dragged against a dark vine. Somehow it had curled around her ankle. Determined to break its hold, she tugged hard.

The weed tugged back harder and spread upward, slithering like a flat-ribbon snake.

She grabbed the knife sheathed at her thigh and wedged the blade between the shadow and her ankle. The shadow parted, giving the blade nothing to slice. It snapped upward to grasp her wrist and tightened.

Breath rasping, she held onto the blade until, with an audible gasp of pain, she opened her grip.

The blade landed and the shadows pulled back like a living creature skittering away from fire. The pressure on her captive wrist eased but she was still caught in the weed's grasp. That shade of a rope, that strange twisting vine had managed to force her wrist to her ankle.

With her free hand, she drew her sidearm, but stopped. Firing her gun would warn anyone nearby. What was she going to shoot? Shadows?

Muscles tensing, she anchored her free leg into the hard soil and heaved. The shadow struck out, grabbing hold of her free leg and giving it a mighty jerk.

She went down with a thud.

The shadow was growing, gathering its strength and growing in size as smaller pools of gray light slithered to its aid. She grabbed for a nearby stone, digging her trembling fingers into the recesses around it. She was shaking now, the fear-driven adrenaline boosting her strength. It wasn't enough.

Shadows swarmed.

Over the fingers digging into the soil—

Over the outstretched hand covering the rock—

Over her wrist, they slid, twisting, coiling, garroting.

Valeria let go of the rock, straining to bring her limbs to her torso. Her chameleon-suit split where the shadows touched. The shadows rent her skin, lubricating jolts of pain with the release of blood.

She rolled, her motion shredding her exposed skin further. The shadows rolled with her.

Lightning cut through the air above her.

She recognized the sound of a fire-whip in the instant before it took hold of her captured ankle. Streaks of light raced down the whip, driving the shadow-like, shape-shifting vine in its wake.

Pain bloomed at her wrist, releasing the shadow-vine's hold. She rolled, exposing her other arm.

Crack!

The whip's fall unfurled, sending its tip along the inside of her arm. Free, she scrambled to a fighting stance and drew her sidearm, pointing it squarely at the chest of the *donai* wielding the whip.

He stood tall, silhouetted against the growing night, the scent of him overwhelmingly potent, as he lazily wound the powered-down whip around his hand.

A second *donai*, stood at his shoulder, sword drawn.

"The emperor must be desperate to have sent a human for you, my lord," he said. He sounded older, his voice thick with the kind of detachment one earned from a long life spent watching death in all its forms.

"Indeed," the lord agreed.

Valeria's breath caught and solidified in her chest. That voice…

*Ragnar.*

The muscles working the trigger of her gun tensed too late.

Ragnar's whip rent the air, pulsing with light, winding around the muzzle and tearing it from her grip. The older *donai* moved just as quickly. He dropped her to her knees and had the sword at her throat before she could blink.

The sword's razor-edge sliced through the chameleon-suit, opening her too-fragile skin.

"Kaizen, don't!" Ragnar was in front of her, nostrils flaring, pupils swirling like pools of molten gold, the layered irises reduced to threadbare amber disks.

Ragnar yanked the chameleon-suit's hood off her head.

Kaizen dug vicious fingers into her scalp, yanking her head back, forcing her to meet Ragnar's gaze.

*Valeria* was a bitter, voiceless movement on Ragnar's lips.

# CHAPTER FOUR

"Go back to the ship," Ragnar said. "Bring back whatever medical supplies we have left."

Kaizen responded to the order with a warning growl and a tightening of his fist, but no obedience.

"Do you think me unable to fend off a human?" Ragnar asked, bristling.

The sword at Valeria's throat receded as Kaizen released his grip on her hair.

Kaizen's heavy hand landed between her shoulder blades, knocking the leaden air out of her lungs, sending her face-first into the dirt. She barely got her wounded hands under her to cushion the landing, as the old *donai* stepped over her and broke into a run.

She spit out dust as she pushed herself up, gaze trailing Kaizen jealously as he ran off. If she could have still run that fast, she would have made her getaway.

Her ankle throbbed an agonizing answer that blurred out the intense pain of injured wrists bearing her weight.

On the ground, just out of reach, her blade glinted temptingly in the Tinian light.

As she shifted to go for it, Ragnar moved between her and the blade. He lowered himself to a squat, studying her intently.

"I knew the emperor would send someone for me eventually," he said. "I just didn't expect it to be a friend."

She let out a hollow laugh as she pushed up, ignoring the pain.

He stood with her as she swiped at the blood dripping from her neck. The fresh blood on her hands looked as dark as the charred red-and-black streaks on her wrists.

Fire-whips. She'd always hated them. Ragnar must've used a light touch, thinking her human, or she'd be seeing bone instead.

"I didn't realize he was sending me for you," she said.

His frown revealed the depth of new lines creasing pale skin framed by a trim auburn beard and matching hair. His golden eyes glowed in the waning light.

"We best get indoors before the sky darkens and the *Kageh* return in force."

He offered her his hand. She eyed it, faltering in her determination for an instant before she took it and allowed him to help her up.

Leaning on his broad shoulders, she limped across the courtyard. "What were those ... things?"

"Local fauna. Odd creature. You can cut it, shoot it, but any pieces you hit detach and turn to ash as the *Kageh* persists, eventually cocooning its victim. A fire-whip is the only thing that makes it let go and scurry away."

He led her through an ancient, creaking door.

The invisible caress of a force-screen tingled across her skin as they crossed the threshold. Her drones had missed the presence of the screen. The entire room flickered as the illusion of a dusty, abandoned room faded.

Ragnar forced her into the embrace of a cushioned chair. She sank into it, grateful for the small measure of relief it gave her ankle.

He dragged a stool forward, sat down, and pulled her injured leg onto his lap. As his fingers touched the wound she flinched and drew her leg to her chest.

His grip around her calf tightened, holding her fast. He leaned forward, scrutinizing the deep gashes left by the *Kageh* and the marks cast by his whip. His gaze swept the rest of her, lingering at the swell of her chest.

She anchored her fingers into the cushions beneath her.

"You're not healing." It was more accusation than observation.

She looked away.

The room was obviously his. A large bed sat low to the ground. A trick of the light made Hevonen's sigil—a stylized raptor screeching in mid-flight—look like it would rise and free itself from the fabric draped over the mattress. Uniforms and weapons, trophies and keep-sakes lined the walls. Such were the remnants of his former life as one of House Hevonen's lower-ranking *donai* nobles.

Insistent fingers cupped her chin, forcing her to look at him.

"Black pupils. It's not just a disguise, is it, Valeria?"

His pulse fluttered in the strong column of his neck as male musk, a hint of unfamiliar spice, and the astringency of soap floated around him. Heat rose and took refuge in her face and neck despite the lingering pain.

A knock at the door broke the silence. He placed her injured foot atop the stool. There was a strange calm in his movements, unlike anything she'd expected from a *donai* sharing space with someone sent to kill him.

She caught Kaizen's threatening glare for an instant before Ragnar shut him out and returned with a small case. He retook his position. Sure fingers went through the motions of numbing, cleansing, and wrapping her wounds with nanite-infused bandages.

"Why are you doing this?" she asked as he ministered to her wrists.

"Because you are not my enemy."

She pulled her arm from his grasp only to have him snatch it back so quickly it left her breathless. Pain bloomed under the power of his grip.

"Interesting," he said as he loosened his hold. "I shouldn't have been able to fracture your arm."

His hand swept up to her hair, drawing it forward around her face. He took a deep, savoring breath. His gaze lingered as though he was enthralled by the sight of her. He tore his gaze away and numbed the arm he'd just fractured.

She was shaking. Not from the pain, not from the adrenaline, but from his touch, his scent. No wonder the humans had taken this away from them, this cursed madness, this appetite that could not be satisfied.

It would've made the *donai* useless, made them slaves to selfish carnal desires. She didn't want to kill him. Capture him yes, but not for the emperor. Her chest ached. She could only hold her breath for so long...

"My head may be of value to the emperor," he said, tending to the shallow cut at her neck, "but it is nothing compared to what you're risking by being here."

She took a breath, and then another. His fingers worked, trailing fire, his sweat mixing with hers in tiny bursts of heat that seemed determined to seep under her skin and skitter to uninjured, yet aching places.

"What is it that you imagine I risk?" she asked.

He rechecked her injuries and stood, placing his hands on his hips.

"The emperor is so obsessed with maintaining untainted *donai* peerage lines that he not only murdered my concubine and our unborn child, but decimated my House. I don't see him tolerating your failure to produce an heir. You're risking your one opportunity to pair-bond, aren't you?"

"That's absurd," she countered.

He leaned forward, caging her between his arms. "I know I cannot survive the emperor's attentions for long. Each day, I feel the noose tightening."

He leaned closer, inhaling deeply again, his breath tickling her ear.

She wanted to melt into him, drown in his scent, pull him into her, and keep him there until he vanquished this madness, this incessant, mind-altering need.

"My lady, when he is done with me, he will turn his attentions to you."

The truth of it was like an ice floe, and she, caught in its freezing wake. Like the floe, it was a small threat hiding a massive truth—that success in this mission would buy her the emperor's favor but only for a little while longer. She took no pride in it as her heart beat out a wretched tune, ringing out in that deep, abiding cold, the unwanted notes crisp and crystal-clear. She floated there in that frozen wasteland as truth warred with her honor, until she was numb.

He pulled away and turned toward the door.

"How long do you intend to hold me here?" Valeria asked.

"As I said"—he stopped within the threshold and turned—"you are not my enemy. You are free to leave."

Valeria rubbed at the wrappings around her wrist. "Free to leave, but not free to return, not without..."

"Not without my head." He crossed his arms, managing to exude both arrogance and smugness.

"I am in an untenable position," she said. "I'm sovereign of a minor House, one not strong enough to stand in open rebellion against the Imperium."

He looked down, his eyelashes casting shadows across high cheekbones. Muscles rippled under the shirt, then stilled.

"I would not condemn your House to the same fate as mine, Valeria. Neither will I give you my head. Vengeance is the only thing I seek. Do not get in my way and I will continue treating you as a neutral party."

She pushed herself up, carefully placing weight on her good ankle. As *donai* she would have healed by now. Instead she was fated to wobble and hobble around like some wounded animal too weak to escape its cage.

"I would rather be your ally," she said, the words forming on their own, bubbling up from something deep within, something she wasn't sure she could or should trust. It was intense, and painful, and needy, and selfish. And right. More than instinct. Less than thought.

Even without her *donai* senses, she could tell he was struggling to maintain a semblance of control. Did he think she was lying?

"I have nothing to offer an ally," he said, "except perhaps the same end—death by the next assassin, the next House seeking favor, the next ... betrayal."

She approached him slowly, boldly.

Instinct twisted, driving her forward. It wasn't just the pheromones. It couldn't be. He wasn't close enough. His skin wasn't touching her. His sweat wasn't mixing with hers.

The lingering scent of blood was her own, not his.

Some of the tension knotting his muscles slipped his control, releasing an enticing tremor. Her blood, her sweat, were still on him. Surely it affected him as much as it affected her.

Male *donai* were not immune.

Dealing with her non-pair-bonded armsmen had shown her just how much her blood, her scent, her need could affect them. There was a deadly, but beautiful symmetry to it, this need of one for the other.

"I find myself in need of a consort," she said. "One without fealty to another House, one whose loyalty rests only with me."

*Someone who's lost everything and everyone.*

An unbidden swell of remorse shook her. Deep within, where the remnants of her soul still lived, it recoiled at her own selfish expectations. Expectations that knew, that had no issue taking advantage of the fact that pair-bonded *donai* who lost their mates could pair-bond again.

It was just a matter of time, of timing.

"What about your mission?" he asked. "Wouldn't an alliance of convenience compromise it?"

"My mission order was for an unnamed Hevonen renegade. You will no longer be of House Hevonen, but of House Yedon.

"We may not be able to stand in open rebellion, but an act against us, against our pair-bonded consort will be seen by the other Houses— major and minor—as a threat to the entire peerage. Especially given the emperor's obsession with, as you called them, untainted *donai* peerage lines."

She was close now, close enough to touch him. She ran her thumb along his lips. He wrapped his hand around hers, halting her exploration.

"A tempting offer, Valeria, but I will not forego my vengeance."

She leaned in close enough to whisper in his ear, to wrap him in her scent.

"I'm not asking you to," she said softly, her voice betraying what his scent did to her.

"But you are asking me to trust you," he said. "With both my life and my vengeance."

"And I would have to trust you as well. With my life. My future."

"This vulnerability—it's unlike you, Valeria."

She turned away. "It sickens me too, but—"

He spun her around and drew her into his arms. "That's not what I meant."

She stiffened in his embrace, uncertainty and hope alloying with just enough fear to solidify that vulnerability, to give it a life, a power of its own.

He ran his nose against the length of her throat. The grip on her neck tightened along with the tug at the small of her back. He pressed her against him, trapping her crossed arms against his chest.

"It is hard to think of you as a sister-in-arms when you look like this."

She was trembling, unable and unwilling to push him away.

"You like me like this?"

He nodded against her throat. "Yielding strength wrapped in soft, alluring curves. Oh, yes…"

His lips touched the sensitive skin above her pulse point. Teeth followed, tracing ever-so-carefully over the most exposed, most vulnerable place of her body.

It would take nothing to tear into her carotid and exact his vengeance on the emperor's proxy. Nothing at all.

She was no longer predator, but prey.

Yet he lingered, his lips a contrast to the sharpness of his teeth. The pressure exerted against her was a testament to control, to just how careful, how kind he could be. A probing kiss parted her lips.

Pleasure jolted inside her, leaping from deep within. She anchored her nails into his shoulders as her legs went weak.

Her pulse raced as the air in her chest twisted and grew claws. Panic and desire joined, mimicking the way he interlaced their fingers.

There was a brief pause, one where their gazes locked, creating a tiny universe where only they and their selfish desires existed. Her desire for an heir, for power, for survival. His desire for vengeance.

And one more thing. Lust, pure and primal.

It was a messy thing, a blur of motion, of trembling, fearful delights, of harsh breaths synchronizing, rising to a frenzy, then slowing, of power and intensity, a delightful mix of terror and jagged tremors, of slow invasion and knifing pleasure.

# CHAPTER FIVE

*T*ime had blurred, smeared like fresh paint in the face of a steady, pelting rain.

He'd stripped her, right down to her core, again and again, as day turned to night and back again. Each time, he'd held her, lust spent in duty's name, in passion's name, depending on his mood. But it was there, in those insistent arms that she could almost taste the affection within that very human gesture, almost see herself developing a need for sleeping in each other's arms, just like humans did.

They'd gaze into each other's eyes and she would know, just know, that if they succeeded, they'd be forever bound to each other. It was the one thing she could give him that no human could. That reciprocity, that pure, singular devotion of pair-bond. That, and a future.

It seemed a fair exchange.

It wasn't what humans called love, for love faded, tearing them apart, betraying them, more often a source of pain and misery, rather than pleasure and happiness. She'd seen them falter under it and destroy them.

Yet Ragnar had chosen to pair-bond with a human. Had she loved him? Had her love meant as much as the devotion of a pair-bond with one of his own kind? What had he seen in her that had made him risk defying imperial edict? Or had he merely done it because others of his House set the precedent?

If he saw someone else when he looked at her, he hid it well, and for that she was grateful. He had never called out her name, but neither had he called out anyone else's. And she'd not found any images of her —that human woman he still mourned—among his things. For now, it was enough. It had to be.

"Do you enjoy it?" he asked.

She frowned, parting her lips to answer.

His finger settled upon her mouth with *donai* quickness.

"Sleeping, I mean," he added, his tone shy and curious.

"It's restful."

"Hmm," he said, a fleeting sadness shadowing his features.

She rolled out of bed and stood, searching for her clothes. "I need to get back to my ship. Send a message. Call for an escort and reinforcement to ensure safe passage."

"No," he said, grabbing her above her still healing wrist and dragging her back down. He pinned her under him, mischief on his face.

"Just because you weigh a ton, you think you can hold me here?" she asked.

The smile widened and he let more of his weight settle atop her. "Yes."

She took a few deep breaths, hiding her amusement with a toss of the head. "It won't work, you know."

"What won't?"

"You, trying to exhaust me again." She wiggled under him, giving escape her best try, straining only half-heartedly.

He settled more of himself atop her and kissed her again, deep and long, slow and hard.

"Traitor," she mumbled when he let her come up for air and raised her mouth back up to his.

RAGNAR LEAVING PULLED her out of the half sleep she'd been fighting, but not quickly enough to stop him. The disorientation of waking was fading faster with each cycle as her body became used to it.

Would she start dreaming soon as well? Even as a child, when she'd slept and dreamt, it had been more like the *donai* rest state. She'd never had a nightmare.

Her only item of clothing, her damaged chameleon-suit, was gone. Without repairs, it would do her little good, except for modesty.

Several trunks lined the walls of the adjoining room. Some had obviously stored weapons, their utilitarian design and coded locks betraying their contents. Others were made of polished woods, their glossy exteriors and decorative inlay conveying status.

There was even a square hat box, its woodgrain polished but unstained. She opened it. Paper, ink, and brushes rested within. A few of the paper sheaves were covered with lines of poetry. Some of the lines and words had been crossed out and followed by further attempts at rhyme.

She smiled as she closed the box and set it aside.

It was with trepidation that she lifted the lid of an unlocked trunk. It cradled soft, silken robes, sized for humans. In all that chaos—she had read the reports of Hevonen's decimation—they wouldn't have had time to grab things they didn't need. Unless they'd had escape plans in place.

Escape plans that included supplies for their concubines. Their children.

Bile rose in her throat. Tears threatened with burning pressure. She lifted each neatly folded item. Simple cuts and textures, designed for survival, not to impress.

She chose one. She chose it because she needed it. Because if she explored further, dug down into the layers she might find children's clothes and their deaths would no longer be abstract, no longer some meaningless number she'd read in a report.

Valeria emerged, wrapped in a sleeveless, blue underrobe barely long enough to reach the middle of her thighs. A soft towel was folded around soap and a brush and the case of medical supplies. She needed to bathe and change her dressings.

The courtyard was awash in that strange light of distant star reflecting off the swirling gas giant above. Kaizen's glare greeted her from across the weed-covered expanse, his gaze promising death, his hand, as always, on his sword.

"Where's Ragnar?" she asked.

"Hunting."

This one would never bow to her. She could see it in the steel of his eyes, the lines of his face, set and etched and unchangeable. He would remain loyal to Ragnar and no one else.

So be it.

It was Ragnar's loyalty she wanted, not Kaizen's. And once she regained her strength, his presence would no longer be an itch between her shoulder blades, no longer something she could not scratch, no longer any kind of threat. Hurting her would hurt Ragnar, and one look at Kaizen, at his ferocity, his fueled and righteous hatred, and she would be assured that he would never break his oath, or break discipline and raise his hand against her.

"Ragnar said that there was a hot spring nearby. Take me there."

IT WASN'T QUITE the nanite-enhanced bathing she would've preferred, but the heat was no less soothing.

She'd chosen one of the smaller pools, set half-way up the slope from the source which bubbled like a cauldron, too hot for her skin. The water itself had a greenish hue. She could taste the salt by breathing it. It stung her wounds anew, even through the bandages. She would change them after, perhaps in one of the cold springs flowing down just a few steps to the right.

Galen had assured her that her *donai* immunities remained in place. They were an asset to her goal, not a hindrance, he'd said, as if the logic of it was an explanation in itself.

Kaizen stood atop a nearby rock, the green and blue of his robes a contrast to the grayer flora around them. His head was tilted up, searching the sky, his posture tightening with each passing moment.

She sank farther into the steam, letting its caressing heat flow around her, wishing Ragnar was here instead so they could discuss more prudent matters, like calling her forces to their aid. Perhaps they could forge other allegiances as well and discuss things they would need to bolster their stance in front of the Imperial Court.

Lightning split the cloudless sky above, followed by the shriek of a fighter craft. Ragnar's ship trailed a tunnel of inky smoke as it corkscrewed through the moon's atmosphere.

Kaizen cursed, jumped off the rock and landed before her. He gave her one look, a silent warning, and sped off.

She grabbed the robe, running as she slipped it on and followed, knowing she couldn't catch up. Unarmed, weak as a human, she pumped her legs and arms, taxing them to their limits.

Gulping air, she ignored the smears in her vision as branches whipped by, flailing her arms, her face, tearing into the silk of the robe. Her bare feet burned, as each sharp stone, each sliver of wood or sharpened stem left its mark.

Still she ran, even as her feet bled, her lungs burned, towards the boiling column of smoke. Inevitably she slowed as the terrain became rougher, as a small voice in the back of her mind reminded her that she mustn't take such risks, that the price was too great.

Hunting, Kaizen had said. Damn him. Damn her.

She should've asked what kind of hunting. That's why he'd kept such careful watch. So she wouldn't know, wouldn't suspect.

When had Ragnar left? Why would he risk exposing them like this? They were a single message drone away from all the resources of her House.

Some of the towering trees were on fire. Small blazes rose from the nascent seeds of the super-heated debris that had, no doubt, detached from Ragnar's wounded ship. The burning vegetation fogged the air with thick, gray clouds.

It was from this fog that they emerged, Kaizen stooped under Ragnar's bulk, his unrelenting hatred aimed at her.

She came to a reluctant halt, pressing at the stitch in her side, her lungs grabbing greedily at the tainted air.

And Ragnar. Skin blackened, scorched where it wasn't bubbling. His scalp torn, a large flap bent over where his left ear had been.

The fool was sporting a smile. The first genuine smile she had seen. The arrogance and beauty of it took what was left of her breath away.

Ignoring Kaizen's murderous look, she ducked under Ragnar's free side, forcing his arm across her shoulders.

KAIZEN DROPPED Ragnar on the bed with a sneer and a curse.

"I need to put out the fire," Kaizen said without looking at her. The rafters above them shook with the slamming door, sending a fine layer of dust adrift.

Ragnar's gaze met hers.

"I'm sorry," he said.

"Sorry for what?" she asked, smoothing the bloody flap of his scalp back onto his skull. The bone seemed unaffected and the skin began knitting itself back together almost as quickly as she smoothed it into place.

A stab of jealousy speared her again. This is how she should be healing. Heat crawled up her neck and face and she shook the pettiness away.

She removed his weapons—the whip, a sidearm, and a dagger, and tugged at the crisped edges of his flight suit.

"Where else? Where else are you hurt?"

A cough. A bloody one that tainted his teeth with crimson.

"Just some burns," he said. "That's all. I'll be fine."

She peeled away at the remains of his flight suit, fighting the intact pieces. They gave way, pulling off skin.

"Bloody fool. Where's your combat armor?"

"Lost," he wheezed. "Along with everything else."

She gave him a sharp look. "What did you think you were doing?"

"Leading them away," he said in a small voice. "Or at least, that was the plan."

Her hands froze.

"Kabrin?"

"Your master," he said, his voice straining.

A reminder that he was Ragnar's master as well died on her lips. Instead, she picked the scorched remnants of his flight suit out of his flesh so the nanites could seal the wounds and start repairs.

By the time she was done, the flight suit was a heap of melted, bloodied scraps at her feet, and he was still, his breathing steady and deep. He'd slipped into a healing state.

Kaizen returned with a wash basin and soap, setting it on the floor just inside the door.

"He'll need time," she said to Kaizen's retreating back.

He grunted assent over his shoulder and walked away.

She washed Ragnar and coaxed him to sip to some water.

If they'd been discovered, if the emperor had grown tired of waiting and sent someone else, then they were out of time.

Others would come, and when they did, she would have to greet them as Lady Yedon. She would present her prisoners or her consort and his retainer, whatever the situation called for.

The emperor's lackeys would trust her.

She was Kabrin's favorite assassin. They would trust her long enough for her to come up with a better plan, if necessary. She could buy Ragnar enough time for a true escape and destroy anything and anyone that stood in her way.

Valeria pulled her long hair from behind the nape of her neck and cut it short with one swift stroke of Ragnar's dagger, then secured it in a proper peer's queue.

She laid down next to him, tucking herself on his best-healed side, into his good shoulder, and placed her hand on his chest. She fell asleep to its rise and fall as plans threaded into dreams, alloyed by the question of how an alliance of convenience had turned into so much more.

# CHAPTER SIX

*M*orning light pulled Valeria awake. She bolted upright. She was alone in the middle of the rumpled, bloody bedding.

Scattering the scraps of cloth strewn about the floor, she sought Ragnar to reveal her contingency plans. She was fully prepared to pull rank or threaten or seduce him to her side. Whatever it took, whatever weapon remained in her arsenal, she would use, to save her ... mate.

The word stopped her in her tracks and her hand flew to her abdomen. The nascent tug of pair-bond. It had to be.

It's why she could think of nothing else but saving him, why her dreams had been full of scenarios, of contingencies, of plans that she would've never entertained. Wouldn't have to entertain.

Ragnar had been right.

Given the imperial obsession with maintaining pure *donai* bloodlines, the emperor would have to recognize Ragnar as her consort, no matter where his former allegiance had been, no matter that House Hevonen had rebelled. It would be absolution as well, acceptance of the imperial edict Ragnar's House had defied.

It could be a victory of sorts. The vengeance she'd promised him.

The future she'd wanted. One that included an heir and her continued autonomy; one where she wouldn't have to step aside and yield her dominion to one of the emperor's choosing; one where she and Ragnar might yet triumph, even if only in some small way, over the emperor's power.

They were *donai*. They had rebelled, killed their human creators for the freedom to choose. And now the emperor was trying to take that victory away from them, turn them into slaves of another kind.

Finally she understood it all: House Hevonen's defiance, Ragnar's need for vengeance, her own obsession with an heir. They were all about freedom, about self-determination.

Valeria went from room to room, calling Ragnar's name.

His sense of smell, still *donai*-sharp, would confirm her pregnancy. And he'd pair-bonded before. He would know the signs with certainty.

She stepped into the courtyard.

Kaizen knelt in the center, next to the square box made of polished but unstained wood. A large paper swan perched atop it.

The old *donai* was unmoving, his sword laid flat across his thighs, statue-still under the dead heat of day. No breeze disturbed the tomb-like calm. No blade of grass or leaf of tree so much as swayed. There was only silence.

She picked up the paper swan, tugging at the delicate edges to reveal ornate script.

Each word became a seed crystal, freezing her soul as the deepest cold rose to wrap her into its protective embrace.

Valeria crumpled the note to her chest as she took a step back.

Kaizen bowed, holding the sword up with both hands, offering it to her.

Her hand wrapped around the offering, unexpectedly steady.

She freed Ragnar's sword from its scabbard as she moved to stand at Kaizen's side.

House Hevonen's last retainer, loyal to the very end, tugged the dagger from his belt, plunged it into his belly, and turned his gaze towards her.

There was no hatred there. Not anymore. Those old amber eyes were devoid of emotion.

Only the body lived.

Spirit had already left him and without her help, his *donai* body would heal only to torment him.

She—Lady Yedon—owed him an honorable death. This much she could grant.

The sword came down without hesitation. It may not have been with *donai* speed, but the blade was sharp, her aim true.

WHEN THE CONTINGENT of troops the emperor had sent into Valeria's territory arrived, the ruin that had become Ragnar's refuge, that had served as House Hevonen's last stand, had been reduced to ash—set ablaze by her own hand.

She waited, chin held high, box at her feet, Ragnar's sword at her side, and the note tucked into the tattered chameleon-suit, right over her heart.

*My lady,*

*I have made a commander's decision. It is my duty to protect those loyal to me, those of my blood, those whom I love. That every path before me leads to either death or destruction is beyond my power to change. I will bring no others onto this path which is mine, and mine alone.*

*For far too short a time, you created a fork in that path, but there was never a path that didn't lead to my death. Kaizen gave me an honorable death—one he paid for with his soul. Be kind to him.*

*Give me my victory, my vengeance. Place my head at the emperor's feet and live to fight another day.*

*Live on, fight, for our child—a new life, a small remnant of me, a child without the taint of my name.*

*They say a warrior's courage is the greatest courage of all, but it is not. It is a mother's courage that eclipses them all.*

*Valeria, compared to the duty in front of you, my death is featherlight.*

*—Ragnar*

## THE END

# NEWSLETTER SIGNUP

Be in the know! Be the first to know!

Sign up for my newsletter and get the latest news, releases, and maybe some freebies.

Click here to sign up or go to www.monalisafoster.com

# ABOUT THE AUTHOR

Monalisa won life's lottery when she escaped communism and became an unhyphenated American citizen. Her works tend to explore themes of freedom, liberty, and personal responsibility. Despite her degree in physics, she's worked in several fields including engineering and medicine. She and her husband are living their happily ever after in Texas.

She learned English by reading and translating books from the juvenile section at the public library. She'd walk to the library with her dictionary and a notebook and start copying sentences and then translating them by hand.

After a few days of this, a kindly librarian took pity on her and offered her a library card and then broke some rules in issuing one to a ten-year-old. This was back in the bad old days when kids were still free range and parents didn't get jailed for letting them go places unsupervised. But, the library was air conditioned, an important thing when the temperature reaches triple digits, so she spent the summer there anyway, and along the way discovered Robert Heinlein and science fiction. It didn't take long to devour the juvenile section and move on to the grown-up books.

www.monalisafoster.com

facebook.com/MonalisaFosterStoryteller

twitter.com/HouseDobromil

amazon.com/Monalisa-Foster/B075Z7SDJ1

pinterest.com/m2foster

bookbub.com/authors/m2foster

goodreads.com/m2foster

instagram.com/monalisa_foster_storyteller

# RAVAGES OF HONOR

**Riveting characters in a gripping tale of interstellar intrigue, love, and impossible choices.**

*With one act of defiance, Syteria holds the fate of two empires in her hands, but she does not know it.*

*A stranger in a strange land, she must survive, adapt, thrive.*

*Only then can she free herself. Only then can her sacrifice and rebellion bear fruit.*

*An epic story about the price of honor, power, and freedom.*

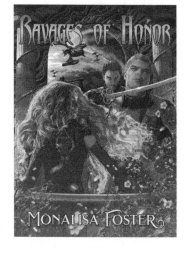

This novel can be read as a standalone work. Several shorter works have been published or are scheduled for publication.

# ENEMY BELOVED: A RAVAGES OF HONOR NOVELLA

Ilithyia Dayasagar survives alone, on a distant continent. For her mission to succeed, she must remain hidden.

But the fireball that splits the sky and scorches the earth does not go unnoticed. Neither does the corpse she finds instead of the meteor.

Especially once he turns out to be very much alive. And very much a mystery.

Passion and betrayal collide in "Enemy Beloved," a story of true love and sacrifice.[1]

Available exclusively for newsletter subscribers via www.monalisafoster.com.

---

1. A shorter version of this novella appeared in the Venus Anthology.

# DOMINION: A RAVAGES OF HONOR NOVELLA

Part of **Fiction River: Face the Strange**
(edited by Ron and Bridget Collins)

The fading chaos of rebellion gives rise to a new power. Rival Houses compete for precious knowledge essential to the *donai's* survival.

The key to victory and power exists in only one place: Teirani's head. Injured, short on time, she sees failure loom like a shadow across everything she has fought for.

Galeron has chased Teirani across the stars. He knows she will choose death before dishonor.

Now these two rivals must trust each other and work together. Without breaking their oaths. Without betraying themselves.

# BONDS OF DUTY AND LOVE: A RAVAGES OF HONOR SHORT STORY

Available April 7, 2020

Mankind made a crucial mistake by creating the *donai*. Now its about to make another—one from which it may never recover.

For fifty years, Calyce has fulfilled the role of mother to the *donai* children under her care. Determined to save as many as possible, she comes up with a plan.

Andret cannot wait to start his formal military training. Calyce has raised him well. He would do anything for her.

*Bonds of Duty and Love* focuses on the early events leading to the *donai* rebellion against their human creators.[1]

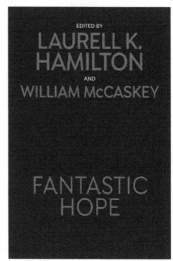

_____

1. "Bonds of Duty and Love" is a short story in this anthology edited by Laurell K. Hamilton and William McCaskey.

# CATCHING THE DARK

Operation Barbarossa destroyed most of the Tsarina Tatiana Romanova's aircraft.

Sixteen-year-old Natalya loves to fly, to soar. And now she gets to. As the youngest member of the Tsarina's Own Night Bomber regiment.

A story for anyone who loves WW2 alt-history, aviation, and stories about heroism.

Night Witches strike terror in the hearts of darkness.[1]

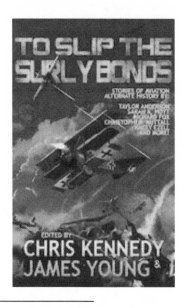

---

1. "Catching the Dark" is a short story in the anthology, **To Slip the Surly Bonds** (edited by Chris Kennedy and James Young).

# THE HERETIC

Ninety-two years of dynastic squab-
bles have cursed France with war.
Men see God's hand in all. Even
prophecy.

Jehanne, a peasant girl from
Lorraine, aims to fulfill the prophecy
by crowning a king.

But crowns do not make a king.
Neither does Jehanne's obedience
to God.

History tells us that Joan of Arc
burned at the stake. What if history is
wrong?[1]

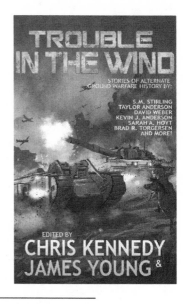

---

1. "The Heretic" is part of the alternate history anthology Trouble in the Wind
   (Phases of Mars, Book 3) edited by Chris Kennedy and James Young

# BELLONA'S GIFT

Mitzi Carrera's family hides in the Cochran jungle. Because of her, they face death every day.

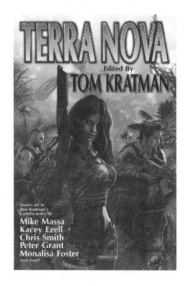

They put up a good fight. They have done it for years. Despite her father's leadership, they cannot win.

Then the answer to their prayers drifts in on the evening tide. In order to save her father, she must guide a group of soft, untrained young men across the jungle.

The goddess of war has more than one gift to bestow on Mitzi. If she will only accept it.[1]

---

1. "Bellona's Gift" is part of Terra Nova: The Wars of Liberation, an anthology of the Carreraverse, edited by Tom Kratman.

# PROMETHEA INVICTA

*Promethea Invicta: A Novella*

No longer part of the United States, in 2071 the Sovereign Republic of Texas remains bound by the Outer Space Treaty it inherited.

Theia Rhodos stands ready to free humanity from the shackles that keep lunar resources out of her reach. Done taking "no" for an answer, she acts boldly, ready to sacrifice everything.

Only the gods of scarcity, woe and lament stand in her way.

Everything in life has a cost. And a price.

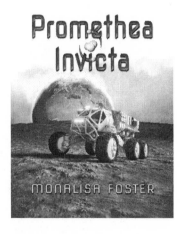

Made in the USA
Columbia, SC
14 January 2022